RULE BOOK #2
How to Fish
for Trouble

D0168663

By Valerie Wilson Wesley
Illustrated by Maryn Roos

JUMP AT THE SUN
HYPERION BOOKS FOR CHILDREN • NEW YORK

For Nandi, Thembi and Cheo
when they were very young.

Text copyright © 2004 by Valerie Wilson Wesley
Illustrations copyright © 2004 by Maryn Roos

Printed in the United States of America

First Edition

1 3 5 7 9 10 8 6 4 2

Library of Congress Cataloging-in-Publication Data on file.

ISBN 0-7868-1807-7

Visit www.hyperionbooksforchildren.com

I, Willimena Thomas, love everything about spring—especially spring vacation. I get to do lots of stuff with my mom and dad. My dad always takes Tina (my older sister) and me fishing. We have the best time.

So when I found out that my favorite cousin Teddy was coming to spend spring break with us, I was so happy. That is, I was so happy until:

My cat had to move to the creepy, moldy cellar.

Tina and Teddy made fun of me.

My dad spent more time with Teddy than with me. We went fishing.

It didn't take long for me to find trouble, make trouble, and stay in trouble, even when I was trying to be good.

So if you're going to get in trouble anyway, here's how to do it step by step. . . .

Willie

My Rules Step by Step

Willimena's
Rules

STEP #1:
Grow Very Big Ears

"Willimena Thomas, you have very big ears for a little girl!" my dad always tells me. He doesn't mean that I really have big ears. My ears are the same size as my sister Tina's. He just means that I hear things I'm not supposed to hear. That's what happened Thursday night.

We had just finished eating dinner. My mom and dad were in the kitchen cleaning up. Tina and I had spelling tests the next day, so they didn't make us help. I was sitting in my favorite corner outside the kitchen door.

My spelling words for the week weren't easy. The hardest one was *frontier*. I couldn't remember where to put the *i*. Was it before or after the *e*? I closed my eyes and tried to picture the word in my mind, and that was when I heard my parents. They were talking about my cousin Teddy. I tried not to listen, but I couldn't help it.

Teddy is my favorite cousin. He's one year older than me, but he never brags about it.

The last time I saw Teddy, he promised he would show me how to fly his kite. He flew it higher than anyone else's in the sky. It made me proud to be Teddy's cousin.

"Next week will be a great time for Teddy to be here," my mom said. "It's spring vacation and school will be out. There will be lots for everyone to do."

"I promised to take Willie and Tina fishing next Thursday," my dad said. "Teddy will really enjoy going to the lake."

I grinned. I love to go fishing with my dad. We get up early, pack a lunch, and always have a good time. My dad was right. Teddy would enjoy fishing, too.

"We have to get ready—he's coming tomorrow," my mom said. "He'll have to sleep in the study, and we'll have to make sure there is no dust around."

"And Doofus Doolittle will definitely have to go into the cellar for the week," my dad said.

My breath got caught in my throat. I couldn't *believe* what I was hearing.

Doofus Doolittle is our cat. He has big

golden eyes that glow green in the dark, and he purrs when he is happy. If he were a girl instead of a cat, he would be my best friend.

I forgot about my spelling words. I forgot that my parents were talking to each other and not to me. I forgot about everything but Doofus Doolittle and what my dad had said.

"No!" I screamed. "You can't put Doofus Doolittle in the cellar! You can't do it! I won't let you!"

My dad put down the dishcloth and turned off the water. "Willie, what on earth are you doing here?" he asked.

"You are supposed to be in your room studying your spelling words," my mom said.

I didn't care. I was too mad.

4

"No!" I said again. "I won't let you put Doofus Doolittle in that terrible place! I don't care if Teddy is coming or not!"

The cellar is the creepiest place in our house. It's always dark, even if the light is on. There are piles of old furniture, moldy clothes, and other stuff nobody wants. Shadows pop up from nowhere. Moss grows on the walls. It smells like wet, dirty sneakers mixed with yesterday's garbage. Tina and I never go down there. It's too scary.

My dad sighed. My mom shook her head sadly. I felt like I was going to cry.

"Let's talk," my mom said.

My mom called Tina to come downstairs. When Tina got into the living room, Mom said, "Dad and I want to talk to you and Willie about something important."

Tina glanced at me. And I just couldn't keep it in any longer.

"Doofus Doolittle is going to have to go into the cellar for a week!" I blurted out.

Tina gasped and stared at my parents. "Why?" she asked.

"Your cousin Teddy is coming for a week," my mom said.

"Whoopee!" Tina said. That's her new word for something that's good. I glared at her. She seemed to have forgotten where Doofus Doolittle was about to go.

"You both know that Teddy has asthma," my dad said. Tina and I nodded that we knew.

"He is allergic to certain things, like dust and milk," my mom said. "They are called triggers, and they can bring on an asthma attack."

"What will happen if Teddy smells a trigger?" Tina asked.

"He can have an attack, and he won't be able to breathe. That's why Teddy always carries his inhaler with him and why he takes his medicine every day," my mom said. She paused and then said, "Sometimes dander can be a trigger, too."

Neither Tina nor I knew what dander was. My mom looked at us and then said, "Dander is like a dust that comes from animal hair."

I sighed hard and long. Doofus Doolittle was an animal, so he must have dander. So being around Doofus Doolittle could make Teddy have an asthma attack.

"When is Teddy coming?" Tina asked.

"He will be here tomorrow morning,

and I want to vacuum the house before he gets here. Doofus Doolittle will have to go into the cellar tonight."

"Okay," Tina said in a small voice. "But I've got an idea, Willie. Let's make Doofus Doolittle a house in the basement."

We found an old blanket and wrapped it around a pillow. I found the little gray mouse that he likes to play with and a little ball of catnip. Then I got my dad's flashlight.

Tina turned on the cellar light and headed down the stairs.

"Willie, you go first since you've got the flashlight," she said.

"No. You're the oldest, you go first," I said. I handed her the flashlight.

"Get behind me," she said as she opened the basement door. I knew she was trying to

sound brave, like she wasn't afraid of anything. We began to walk downstairs. Suddenly there was a deep, rumbling sound coming from the cellar. We both turned around and ran back upstairs. We knew it was the furnace, but it scared us anyway.

That was when my dad came into the kitchen.

"Come on, girls, I'll go down with you," he said, and Tina and I followed him.

We made Doofus Doolittle a little bed. I brought down his water and food bowls and my dad brought his tray of kitty litter. Then I went upstairs to get Doofus Doolittle and took him down into the cellar. Tina and I both tucked him into his new bed.

"Time for both of you to go to bed, too," my mom called out.

"Good night, Doofus Doolittle. We'll see you in the morning," Tina said.

"I'm sorry, Doofus Doolittle," I whispered in his little pointed ear.

Before I went to sleep, I took my journal out of the secret place where

I hide it and wrote,

> I'm out of school next week. My dad is
> taking us on a fishing trip. And even
> though Doofus Doolittle has to go into
> the basement, I'm so happy that Teddy
> is coming.

Then I added,

> I know that next week is going to be a
> great week!

Little did I know just how wrong I was.

STEP #2:
Always Do What Your Baby-sitter Says

I love my cousin's grin. It makes you want to grin back even if you don't feel like grinning. But Teddy's grin wasn't working on Friday afternoon.

Tina and I had just come home from school. Teddy's mom, my aunt Jan, had dropped Teddy off that morning, and Mrs. Cotton, our baby-sitter, was going to stay with us until my parents came home. When Mrs. Cotton is in a good mood, she makes us tasty things to eat, like hot chocolate, cookies, or popcorn. When she's in a bad mood, she's grumpy and complains about her feet.

The moment Tina and I came through the back door, we smelled popcorn coming from the living room! Mrs. Cotton was in a good mood.

"Whoopee!" Tina yelled, and we ran into the living room toward the bowl of popcorn.

Then I remembered Doofus Doolittle. I stopped in my tracks. The popcorn would have to wait. Doofus Doolittle came first.

I went to the cellar door and turned on the light. "Hi, Doofus, I'm home!" I picked him up and hugged him. Even though I was scared of the cellar, I made myself go down all the way. I checked his food and water and fed him the treats I give him when he is good. Then I ran back upstairs.

"Willie, come on and get some popcorn. It's almost gone," Teddy called from the living room. Teddy's mouth was filled with popcorn. Tina was right beside him grabbing it by the handfuls and shoving it into her mouth. The trouble started when I reached for the bowl.

"Stop. Stop this very instant!" Mrs. Cotton said, holding out her hand like a policeman in a cartoon. Teddy stopped chewing. Tina stopped shoving popcorn into her mouth. I stopped reaching for the bowl.

"Were you in the cellar with the little *animal*?" she asked.

"I wanted to give Doofus Doolittle some food," I said in a small voice.

"You were playing with the little animal, so you must wash your hands before you put them in the popcorn bowl!" Mrs. Cotton said.

I knew Mrs. Cotton was right. I ran into the kitchen as fast as I could and rinsed them off. Then I ran back into the living room.

"With soap?" she asked with a scowl.

I ran back into the kitchen, but there was only dishwashing detergent for the dishwasher on the counter. I ran upstairs to the bathroom. There was no soap in the soap dish. Lucky for me, I found a tiny piece in the tub. I scrubbed my hands, dried them off, and ran back downstairs.

"Let me see," Mrs. Cotton said. She examined my hands front and back.

"That's good," she said. "Now you may help yourself to the popcorn."

When I looked in the bowl there was nothing left except a few half-popped pieces. I stared at the popcorn bowl, too mad to say anything.

"Sorry, Willie. I guess Tina and I were hungrier than we thought," Teddy said.

"Will you please make some more popcorn, Mrs. Cotton?" he asked. He gave her a grin. But it didn't work.

"Not now. It's almost time for dinner," Mrs. Cotton said.

That's when Tina gave me a little smile and a wink. She had decided to help me. "Please, Mrs. Cotton. Pretty please," she said, using her nicest voice.

"Please, Mrs. Cotton," Teddy chimed in.

I didn't smile or say anything.

But it didn't matter. Mrs. Cotton was unmoved.

"It's too late, children," she said.

"I understand, Mrs. Cotton," Teddy said.

"Thank you for taking such good care of us," Tina said.

I stared at my sister and my cousin in disbelief. Couldn't Mrs. Cotton see they were just trying to get on her good side?

"You are two very polite children," Mrs. Cotton said. "And I have something very special for each of you." Mrs. Cotton opened her shiny black purse and pulled out a pack of chewing gum. She gave a stick to Teddy and one to Tina. She didn't give anything to me, just because I hadn't put on a fake voice and smiled. I left the room without saying anything to anybody and went back to the cellar to play with

Doofus Doolittle. Even with Doofus in my lap, the more I thought about gum, the sadder I felt. I still felt bad after Mrs. Cotton went home.

"What's wrong, Willie?" my mom asked at dinner.

"Nothing," I said.

"Mrs. Cotton gave me and Teddy gum, and she didn't give any to Willie," Tina said. My mom looked surprised.

"Why didn't Mrs. Cotton give you any gum, Willie?" she asked.

"She said it was because Teddy and I were polite and we deserved it," Tina answered for me.

"Willie, weren't you polite to Mrs. Cotton?" my mom asked.

"I was mad because she made me wash my hands after I played with Doofus

Doolittle, and she made me miss out on popcorn, and because she's a grouch!" I said.

My mom sighed. "Willie, I'm sure Mrs. Cotton didn't mean to hurt your feelings. Maybe if you're polite to Mrs. Cotton, she'll give you a stick of gum next time," Mom continued.

"I don't want any of Mrs. Cotton's rotten gum!" I said. I knew that would probably make my mom mad, but I said it anyway.

"Willie!" There was a warning tone in my mom's voice, and she had a frown on her face. I could tell she meant business.

"I'm sorry," I said.

Before we went to bed, Tina and I stopped in the study to say good night to Teddy. My mom had pulled out the couch and made it into a bed.

On the night table next to Teddy's bed was a photograph of Teddy's dad, Uncle Bill, who doesn't live with Teddy and his mom anymore. Teddy looks a lot like his father. I picked up the photo to look at it.

"That's my dad," Teddy said.

"Do you miss him?" Tina asked.

"Yeah. But I'm going to be seeing him next week, when I get home," Teddy said.

"What's this?" I asked, picking up an object that was shaped like an L.

"My inhaler," Teddy said. "It's filled with medicine that goes right into my lungs in case I start to wheeze."

"Like, if you're having an asthma attack?" Tina asked.

"Yes, if I have an attack, I have to breathe this in and then call a grown-up fast so that I can get help." Teddy took the

21

inhaler and put it back on the table beside his bed.

"Tina, Willie, Teddy, everybody in bed, now!" my mom called from the bottom of the stairs.

"See you tomorrow, Teddy," Tina said, heading into our room.

"'Night, Tina. 'Night, Willie," Teddy said. As I was getting ready to leave, Teddy placed something in my hand.

It was the stick of gum that Mrs. Cotton had given him earlier.

"I don't like gum that much," he said with a Teddy grin. I gave him a hug, then popped the gum into my mouth and chewed it fast, even though I'd just brushed my teeth.

STEP #3:
Get Mad at Everyone

It was Saturday. The best day of the week. When we went outside, it was so warm, all we needed to wear were sweaters. I was feeling so good, I let Tina borrow my favorite sweater. My grandma knitted it for me last year. It's purple, one of my favorite colors. The only problem is that it's way too big for me. But it fits Tina now, so when she wants to borrow it, I usually let her. So Tina wore my purple sweater, and I put on my green one, and we headed to the perfect place for perfect days: the Greenes' backyard.

My best friend, Amber, and Tina's best friend, Lydia, were coming out of their house just as we were leaving ours.

"Who is that?" Amber asked, pointing to Teddy as she skipped across the grass to meet us.

"I'm Teddy. I met you last summer," Teddy said.

"I remember you now! This is my sister, Lydia," she said. Lydia isn't as nice as Amber. She doesn't warm up to new people easily. Sometimes she's friendly. Sometimes she's not. Teddy held out his hand to give her a handshake. She stared at his hand for a couple of seconds like she was counting his fingers. Then a grin spread on Teddy's face. It worked like a charm.

"Welcome to the neighborhood, Teddy,"

she said as she gave his hand a hearty shake. I breathed a sigh of relief. If Lydia was friendly to Teddy, I knew everybody else probably would be, too.

The Greenes' backyard is the best backyard I've ever been in. It's probably the best backyard in the world. Maybe even the universe, if they have backyards in the universe. It is four times as big as anybody else's backyard.

But the best thing about the Greenes' backyard is the bright blue merry-go-round that sits smack in the middle. It doesn't have horses or ducks like the carousels in amusement parks. And doesn't have a motor that makes it go round by itself. It runs on "people power," Mr. Greene says. Somebody has to hold the bars and run as fast as he or she can.

Sometimes, when Mr. Greene is around, he pulls it. When he's at work, Gregory Greene, the oldest kid in the Greene family, will do it.

Teddy had never visited the Greenes' backyard before. Today was his first time.

I could tell that Teddy was excited and a little scared as the five of us headed into the yard. He put his inhaler in his pocket, but he kept a steady hand on it.

"Don't worry, Teddy, you'll be okay," I whispered to him. I knew that there would be a lot of kids there because it was a Saturday. He gave me a Teddy grin, and said he was okay.

I was right. When we walked into the Greenes' backyard, everybody was there. Even Booker, the youngest kid on the block. He was on the merry-go-round with his sister, Betty. Gregory Greene was holding the bars and getting ready to pull.

"Let's ride!" he called out, running as hard as he could. He jumped on when it was spinning as fast as a top!

George, Gregory's brother and my enemy, was hitting a tennis ball against the side of his house.

Pauline, my next-to-best friend, was sitting on a cushion in the center of Mrs. Greene's garden. She was reading a story to Grace Greene, who next to the baby, Ginger, is the youngest Greene kid. Candy, the teenager who watches Pauline, was pouring grape drink into paper cups for anybody who wanted to have some. Candy mixes the best grape drink I've ever tasted.

Lena and Lana, the twins who live

down the street, were sitting under a big willow tree playing cards.

Teddy stood at the edge of the yard, taking everything in. His eyes were big, and his mouth was open. He looked like he wasn't quite sure what to do or say first.

I could see he was holding his inhaler tight, like he was afraid he might lose it. Gregory saw him looking. He got off the merry-go-round and came to where we were standing.

"Hey, kid. Wanna ride?" he asked Teddy.

"Sure!" Teddy ran over to the merry-go-round. Gregory made it stop, and showed Teddy how to hold on tight. Then he twirled it around, until it was going so fast that Teddy's red-and-white-striped shirt was a blur. When it stopped, Teddy, Booker, and Betty all jumped off. They fell on the ground, laughing and dizzy.

"Hey, you're a big kid. You can handle this. You want to pull for a while?" Gregory asked Teddy after the fourth ride. You usually had to visit the Greenes' backyard at least six times before Gregory would let you pull. Teddy flashed Gregory one of his grins, and took over. Gregory had only let me pull once.

Every time I looked, Teddy was having a good time. He had made friends with everybody. He pulled Booker and Betty on the merry-go-round until they were too dizzy to stand up. When George found out that Teddy knew how to play tennis, he asked Teddy to show him a couple of strokes.

When Pauline grew tired of reading to Grace, Teddy took over and read her her favorite stories. Teddy helped Candy

pour grape juice. He played checkers with Amber and cards with Lena and Lana. By the end of the day, he was everybody's best friend.

I, on the other hand, was having a terrible time. When I tried to ride on the

merry-go-round, I fell off and skinned my knee. When nobody was looking, George hit me with a tennis ball. Candy ran out of grape juice by the time she got to me. That brought back all my bad feelings about the day before and the popcorn. Lydia and

Tina were telling secrets that they didn't want me to hear. Amber was having such a good time playing checkers with Teddy that she didn't want to play with me. Finally, I played cards with Lena and Lana, but I lost every hand.

By the end of the day, I was glad to go home.

"Your cousin is great!" Gregory said as we were leaving.

"Teddy is so-o-o nice," said Lena and Lana together. "Can he come back tomorrow and play with us?"

Then George said something that really made me feel bad. "Hey, Tina, your cousin is really cool. Why don't you trade your dumb sister in for him?"

Tina laughed like it was a big joke.

Sometimes when I'm mad I do things that I shouldn't. I was mad because everybody had had a good time that day but me. I was mad because Tina had laughed at George's joke about trading me in. I wanted to take it out on somebody. That somebody was Tina.

"Give me back my sweater!" I said to her, as we were walking back to the house. Tina looked surprised.

"No!" she said.

"It's mine. I want it back!"

"No!" Tina said. "You said I could wear it, and I am!"

"I want it back now!" I said.

"Then take back your ugly old sweater!" Tina said. She took it off and threw it on the ground. "You're being mean, Willie. George is right. I wish I could trade you in!"

"I wish I could trade you in, too!" I said as I picked my sweater up from the ground, dusted it off, and put it on over my green one. It didn't make me feel any better.

And I was about to feel worse.

STEP #4:
Learn How to Pout

"Do you want to play the alphabet game, Teddy?" Tina asked Teddy as we were walking down the street to our house.

"Sure," Teddy said.

I knew that Tina's feelings were hurt because I had taken back my sweater. But I wasn't about to apologize.

My dad taught us the alphabet game. It's kind of like playing Scrabble without a board. You start with *A* and you name all the good—or bad—things that begin with that letter. *A* is easy. I can always think of

lots of things that start with *A*, like *apples*, *acorns,* and *apricots*. *Z* is harder. *Q* is impossible. Usually we start with *A*, but sometimes we start with another letter. Tina started with *T*.

"Can you think of terrific words that start with *T*?" she asked Teddy. "I have two things, *Teddy* and *Tina*." She and Teddy giggled.

"What about *tasty*?" asked Teddy.

"That's good. How about *tops* and *tender*?" Tina said.

"Don't forget *Thanksgiving*, *thank you*, and *treasure*," Teddy said, getting into the game.

"That's good. How about *tutu*? Grandma gave me a pink tutu for Christmas and I love to wear it," said Tina. "I love *trombones* and *tulips*, too."

"I like *tea*," said Teddy. "Especially with honey in it."

"I've got some *T* words for you. How about *terrible, trouble,* and *tornado*?" I said. Neither Tina nor Teddy seemed to hear me.

"And don't forget *toys* and *tapioca*," Teddy said.

"I don't like *tapioca*, but I love *taffy, turkey*, and *treats*."

"Aren't we lucky our names begin with *T* instead of *U* or *Z*?" Tina asked.

Teddy nodded that he was.

"Or *W*," Tina added with a glance in my direction. "Can anybody ever think of good words that begin with *W*?"

My mind went blank. I couldn't think of anything—good or bad—that started with *W*, to save my life.

"How about *wacky*, *wicked*, and *weasel*!" Tina said. Both she and Teddy started to laugh.

"How about *weird*, *wild*, and, don't forget, *worm*!" he added.

"Ooh! Disgusting! I hate worms," Tina said.

"Well, they do begin with *W*," Teddy said and glanced at me.

All I could do was poke out my lip, which is what I do when I get mad. It lets people know—like Tina—that they'd better leave me alone. It was bad enough for Tina to tease me, but for Teddy to do it too really made me mad. It was two against one! I poked out my lip when I walked into the house. It was still poked out when I threw my purple sweater on my bed and when I washed my hands and while we helped my mom put the food on the table.

"Willie, what in the world is wrong?" my mom said when we all sat down to dinner. We were having barbecued chicken—my favorite meal—the leg is my favorite part. Usually that makes me smile. Today it just made my lip go out farther.

My dad looked at me and grinned. "Better pull that lip in before it freezes like that," he said. He always says that whenever I pout. Usually it makes me feel better. A smile always manages to poke itself through. But not tonight.

"Wow, chicken! I love chicken," Teddy said.

"What piece would you like, Teddy?" my mom said as Tina passed him the platter.

"I'll take a leg," Teddy said.

"Help yourself," my mom said.

"Hey! Wait!" I said. But I said it too late.
Teddy had already taken a bite from it.
Tina had the other one on her plate.

"That's not fair!" I said. "I always have
the leg. That's not fair!"

My dad gave me a warning look. "Willie,

Teddy is our guest," he said.

But Teddy wasn't too much of a guest to tease me like my sister had. I poked my lip out so far I could hardly talk.

"First come, first served," said Tina. She took a big bite out of her chicken leg.

"Willie, you can have the wings," my mom said as she put them on my plate. The wings are my next-to-favorite part of the chicken. But a wing is not a leg.

After we had finished I didn't want to talk to anybody, not even my parents. I went down into the cellar to talk to Doofus Doolittle. I felt like he was my only friend in the world that night.

Doofus Doolittle was lying next to the furnace. The minute he saw me he ran over, and I picked him up and hugged him as tightly as I could.

He rubbed his nose up against mine, which always makes me smile. He started to purr. He licked my face, and his rough, little tongue felt so funny against my cheek, it made me laugh. It was the first time I'd laughed since this morning when

I watched cartoons. After a while, I went back upstairs. I still didn't feel like watching TV or talking to anybody, so I got my library book and took it to the corner outside the kitchen door.

When it was time to go to bed, Teddy, Tina, and I walked up the stairs together.

I waited for Teddy and Tina to finish their baths, then I got ready to take mine.

By the time I had finished my bath, I wasn't mad at Tina anymore. I was just sleepy and crawled into bed.

As we lay there in the dark, I thought about the things that had happened that day. I realized that it really wasn't Tina's fault that I hadn't had a good day. But it wasn't fair of Teddy to join in the alphabet game like he had. I hadn't done anything mean to him.

"Tina, are you still awake?" I asked.

"Yeah," she said.

"I'm sorry for taking the sweater back," I said.

"That's okay."

"Willie, you still awake?" Tina asked after a couple more minutes. "Here are some wonderful words that start with *W*. There's *winner*, *wise*, and *waffle*. There's *walnut*, *walrus*, and *wildflower*. There are as many great words that start with *W* as with *T*," she said with a loud yawn.

I smiled when I heard that, but then I thought about something else.

"Tina, would you trade me in for somebody else if you could?" I asked.

But as always, Tina fell asleep, and didn't answer me.

STEP #5:
If You're the Third Wheel, Make It a Bumpy Ride

"Do you like Teddy?" I asked Tina the next morning.

Tina looked surprised. "Of course. Everybody likes Teddy. He is one of the nicest kids I've ever met. Everybody says we're lucky he's our cousin. Don't you like Teddy?"

"Sometimes I don't," I said in a quiet voice.

Tina looked at me. "Willie, that's not nice! He's our cousin. Plus, Teddy really likes you," she said.

I waited a moment before I asked my next question. "If you could trade me in for Teddy, would you do it?"

Tina gave me the look she gives me when I've said something dumb. "You can't trade one person in for another person, Willie. I'm stuck with you!"

That wasn't exactly the answer I was hoping for.

"Even if I could trade you in, I never would, not even for Teddy."

Tina's words made me smile. Saying that she would never trade me in for Teddy made me feel better. But by the time Wednesday rolled around a few days later, I wasn't so sure about my dad.

That was when we went "birding" on South Mountain Reservation.

"Birding" is what my dad calls watching birds. He loves to watch birds. Dad even has a pair of field glasses that he uses to spot them when they fly by, and a little book with pictures of different birds. When he sees a bird, he looks in the book and finds its picture. He gets really excited if the bird is rare or has come from far away.

I think birding is boring. Birds are okay, but they're just a cut above fish on my list of favorite animals. But just my luck, Teddy loved birds almost as much as my dad did.

On Wednesday morning, right after breakfast, my dad took Teddy and me to a special place called the South Mountain Reservation. It has paths for people to walk down to look for different kinds of birds. Tina didn't go because she doesn't like birds that much either. Besides that, Lydia had invited her to go to the movies. I went because I wanted to spend time with my dad. But the only person my dad seemed to want to talk to was Teddy.

"Look at that one," my dad would whisper when a bird would land nearby. He would study the bird through his field glasses. Before we left, my dad had given me an old pair of field glasses, but they felt heavy and awkward around my neck, and I couldn't see out of them. Teddy had his own pair.

"Wow!" Teddy would say. Then he would look up the bird in the book. Then my dad and Teddy would talk about what they had both seen.

I didn't say anything because I hadn't seen anything. And they both seemed to forget that I was there. Now I knew what it felt like to be a third wheel.

My dad had promised to take us to lunch after our trip. I was looking forward to that. But I didn't have a good time there, either. My dad ordered a hamburger with mustard, relish, and onions. Teddy ordered the same thing. I ordered a hot dog with ketchup. But then I wished I had gotten a hamburger, too, just like my dad, even though I like hot dogs better.

When it was time to go home, Teddy tried to get into the front seat with my dad. That was the last straw. Being the third wheel was for the birds.

"No," I said to Teddy. "I want to sit in the front."

"But you sat in the front on the way here," Teddy said.

"He's my dad, not yours. So I get to sit beside him!" I said.

"But that's not fair," Teddy said.

"You have your own dad. Don't try to

steal mine!" I said. Teddy's eyes got big. I was sorry that I had said that. But not sorry enough to apologize.

"Willie," my dad said. His voice was soft. He put his arm on my shoulder. "You sat in the front seat on the way over, let Teddy sit here on the way back."

"You're my dad, not his," I said.

"Willie," my dad said, giving me a warning look. So I sat in the backseat like he said.

I didn't eat much dinner that night. I wasn't very hungry.

"Is everybody ready for the big fishing trip tomorrow?" my dad said when we had finished.

"Whoopee!" said Tina.

"I can hardly wait," said Teddy.

I tried to smile, but it wasn't a real

smile. Even though I had been looking forward to the fishing trip, now I wasn't feeling that excited.

Before I went to sleep, my dad came in and gave me an extra hug. "You're my special little girl," he said when he kissed me good night. "Nobody in the world is as special to me as you are."

That made me feel much better, and I gave him a hug and held him tightly.

"Good night, Tina!" Teddy called out from the study.

"'Night, Teddy!" Tina called back. "Don't forget to bring your good-luck charm tomorrow."

"Good night, Willie," Teddy called out to me.

I didn't say anything, and I didn't care if Teddy's feelings were hurt.

STEP #6:
Obey the Rules

"Rise and shine. Time to catch some fish!" my dad called out. I wasn't ready to get up yet. I'd forgotten what day it was. Then I remembered and opened my eyes.

"Willie! Tina! Teddy! Time to get up!" my dad said again.

"Willie's getting up first," Tina yelled out to my dad. She was going back to sleep.

"That's okay, Tina. You can go first," I said. I was having a hard time keeping my eyes open.

"No, you!" Tina said.

"Stop arguing and get out of bed. The first one up gets to sit in the front seat."

It was so early in the morning, the sun wasn't completely up yet. I yawned one last time. Then I pulled myself out of bed to look for my slippers. If I sat in the front, I could choose the CD that we would play. And I could finally talk to my dad, which I felt like I'd hardly had a chance to do since Teddy had arrived. But I was too late. The bathroom door closed just as I was slipping on my shoes. Teddy had beaten me to the bathroom. He would get to sit in the front with my dad. Again.

I got back in the bed and pulled the covers up over my head. What was the use of getting up now?

When I finally came downstairs, Tina and Teddy were finishing their cereal.

They were talking and laughing. The kitchen was bright with sunshine. Everybody looked wide awake.

"Well, Miss Sleepyhead. I see you finally made it downstairs," my dad said. All I could do was yawn.

I went down to give Doofus Doolittle his food and a hug, and then back upstairs to finish eating my breakfast. Even though it wasn't cold, my dad told us to put on sweaters and heavy pants. He also made us pack our life vests in case we fell in the water.

After we finished collecting our "gear," as my dad called it, Tina and I got out our fishing poles. Some time ago, he made us fishing poles out of bamboo. My dad uses a rod and reel instead of a fishing pole. He puts on high, heavy boots so that he can wade deep into the water to catch fish. Tina and I have to stay on shore. Since Teddy didn't have a fishing pole, my dad gave him one of his old fishing rods. But he told Teddy that he would have to stay on shore with Tina and me.

When everybody was ready to go, my dad reviewed the rules that all good fishermen should follow. Tina and I had heard the rules before. But we listened to them anyway.

Fishing Rule #1: Stay on shore. Lots of grown-ups fish at the lake where we go, and my dad wades away from shore and talks to the other grown-ups. He always keeps an eye on us, but we can never, ever, leave the shore.

Fishing Rule #2: Respect the lake.
We could not throw anything into
the lake like trash or paper. We had
to make sure it stayed clean so the
fish would have a nice place to
live—until we caught them!

Fishing Rule #3: Respect the fish.
The first time I heard this one I
wondered: How can you "respect" a
fish if you're trying to catch it for
dinner? My dad explained that if we
caught a fish that was too small or
out of season, we had to throw it
back. I've never caught any fish, so
I've never had to put any back.

Finally, we were ready to go. It was a
long drive to the lake, and Teddy got to
sit in the front. But we were all so tired,

nobody cared. The moment my dad started driving everybody fell asleep.

While I was asleep, I had a dream that I had caught more fish than anybody else. In my dream, Tina and Teddy were congratulating me. My dad was so proud of me he carried me around the lake on his shoulder.

"My daughter Willie is the best fisherman in the world!" my dad said in my dream. I woke up with a smile on my face. I was sure my dream meant that I would have good luck. Tonight, everybody would be eating fish that I had caught!

"We're here, everybody," my dad called out when we got to the lake. Usually the water is smooth, but sometimes it's choppy. It was smooth today, almost like glass.

My dad put on his fishing gear and helped us into ours. Then he showed Teddy how to use his rod, then he baited Tina's and my hooks.

We all took our places by the lake. My dad has a special log where Tina and I sit. It's close enough to the water so we can put our poles in, but far enough away from it so we won't fall in. We can watch my dad talking to the other fishermen as he casts out his line.

One of the things I love most about fishing is spending time with my sister. When Tina and I fish, there's nothing to argue about and we don't even tease each other. We just sit there on our log with our poles in the water being quiet.

But it was different this time. Tina talked to Teddy instead of me. They didn't do it to hurt my feelings. It was as if they had forgotten I was there.

"This rod is really great. I know I'm going to catch a lot of fish," Teddy said to Tina.

"I caught a fish once, but it was too little. Maybe it's grown up, and it will come back on my line," Tina said to Teddy.

"Have you ever caught a fish?" Teddy asked me.

"No, she never has. Not once," Tina said, like I couldn't answer for myself.

Suddenly a big smile broke out on Teddy's face.

"I got one! I got one!" he yelled out. Tina and I almost dropped our poles. "I think it's a big one!"

I could tell by the way the fish was pulling on Teddy's line that it was big.

"Tell Dad to come and help," Tina said

to me. I ran to the edge of the water and called him to come and help Teddy reel in the fish. My dad ran over and helped Teddy hold the rod. The fish was strong. But he wasn't as strong as my dad.

"Let me help you reel him in, Teddy. I think he might be too big to bring in by yourself," my dad said.

My dad reeled in Teddy's fish. It must have been ten inches long and weighed ten pounds. Teddy gave my dad a hug, and my dad hugged him back.

"Hey, Teddy. I'm proud of you," he said. "This is my nephew Teddy. Quite a fisherman, isn't he?" he said to the men who had been fishing with him.

They were almost the same words he said in my dream. Only he was praising Teddy and not me.

"Wow, that's really a whopper!" one of the men said.

"He wasn't using a pole with that one, was he?" another man asked.

"I was using my uncle's fishing rod," Teddy said with a grin. "I also had my good-luck charm." Teddy pulled out a four-leaf clover in a plastic case, and the men laughed.

"You need good luck to catch a fish like that," one of them said.

"They usually don't swim that close to shore," another man said.

For the next fifteen minutes, Teddy was the center of attention. Everyone talked about Teddy's fish.

"Are you all tired yet?" my father asked, after he'd cleaned Teddy's fish and put it in the cooler with the others he had caught.

My dad had landed three fish, but none was as big as Teddy's.

"Can we fish a while longer?" Tina asked. My dad looked at his watch.

"How about you, Willie? Are you ready to go home?" It seemed like that was the first thing my dad had said to me since we had been here.

"Can we stay a little longer? I want to try to catch a fish, too," I said.

"Fat chance!" Tina said.

"Shut up, Tina!" I said.

"Shut up yourself," Tina said.

"Okay, we'll stay a while longer," my dad said as he headed out to the lake. The three of us went back to our places.

I waited a few minutes for a fish to pull the line. Nothing happened. I closed my eyes and imagined a school of fish

swimming toward my bait. Nothing happened. I waited another five minutes.
Nothing happened, again.

I looked over to where my dad was
standing. One of the men he was standing
next to had just caught a fish. He and
my dad were talking and laughing. I
remembered what my dad's friend had
said when he saw Teddy's fish, about how
most big fish didn't swim close to shore.

And that was when I got my dumb idea.

Step #7:
Pick One Rule
and Break It

If the fish wouldn't come to me, then I would go to the fish. I knew that my dad might be mad at me at first because I broke Rule #1. But he'd be proud of me, too, when I caught a fish as big as Teddy's.

I didn't want to get my clothes wet, so I rolled up my pants as high as they would go. I glanced at Tina and Teddy. Tina was concentrating on catching a fish. Teddy was attaching his good-luck charm to my dad's fishing rod. I took a quick glance at my dad. He was talking with the man next to him. I picked up my fishing pole and I headed into the lake.

The water was freezing cold. It felt as if the lake were filled with ice cubes. I moved away from the shore closer to the middle of the lake where I was sure the big fish swam. I moved slowly at first, and then a little faster to try to stay warm. Maybe it would be warmer the farther I got from shore.

The rocks on the bottom of the lake were very slippery. They felt like they were covered with moss. I would have to slow down. But the soles of my sneakers made walking slippery, too. I almost fell. But I caught myself before I did.

And then something happened that I wasn't expecting. The lake began to get deeper. It had been up to my ankles. Now it was up to my waist. In a moment, it would be up to my chest.

Suddenly, I knew I should go back to shore.

I tried to turn around. But the lake wouldn't let me turn. The water was moving, and it was moving very fast. Every minute, it seemed to be going faster! Then I slipped.

I felt the water enter my mouth and nose. I stood up quickly, but my face and hands were cold, too. I dropped my fishing pole and saw it float down the lake. I thought about grabbing it, but let it go. I was afraid to move. My face felt as cold as ice. I was really scared now.

"Help!" I screamed. "Help!"

The water was creeping higher.

"Help!" I screamed again. I closed my eyes. "Help!"

That was when I felt somebody's arm around my waist. I knew it was my dad even though my eyes were closed. My dad swooped me up just like he used to when I was a little kid. Then he turned around and walked back to the shore. I could tell by how slowly he was moving that the water was traveling fast.

I slowly opened my eyes. Everybody on shore was gathered around, talking. It was just like it had been when Teddy had caught his fish except nobody was smiling or laughing. Everybody looked very worried. One of the men shook his head.

"Hey, kid, you could have drowned," he said to me. "Never, never go into a body of water by yourself. You can't tell how

dangerous a lake is just by looking at it."

"She should have put on her life jacket," another man said and shook his head.

I dropped my head. I felt dumb and careless. And I was still scared.

"What in the world did you think you

were doing?" my dad asked me. "What if you had tripped and fallen? What if—"

My dad didn't finish his sentence. It was the first time I had ever seen my dad look scared. I knew he must be ashamed of me. I glanced at Tina. She looked like she was going to cry. Teddy looked like he was going to cry, too. Tina came over and gave me a long hug.

I had frightened everybody. I had never felt worse in my life. All because I was trying to catch a bigger fish than Teddy had caught.

"Why did you go out there, Willie?" Tina asked.

"I was trying to catch some fish," I said in a small voice. It sounded dumb now, even to me.

"It's time to go home," my dad said.

Nobody disagreed with him this time.

I felt really bad that I had disobeyed my dad's first and most important fishing rule. I had ruined the day for everybody. I didn't have much to say on the way home.

My dad and Teddy cleaned and fried the fish that Teddy caught. I didn't have any appetite. After dinner, Teddy went upstairs to begin to pack his things. He was leaving the day after tomorrow. I wanted to be by myself, so I got a book and went to my favorite corner outside the kitchen door to read.

I heard my parents talking softly about what had happened. It made me feel bad all over again. Then I heard Tina talking to Lydia on the phone.

"Teddy caught a big fish. I would have caught one, too, but we had to come home because Willie disobeyed my dad and almost drowned," I heard her say.

There was nothing else to do but to go upstairs and go to bed. Before I fell asleep my parents came in to talk to me.

"You did a very dangerous thing today. Do you understand that?" my dad said. "Your punishment is that you won't be able to go fishing again this spring or this summer. And maybe not for a very long time after that."

I nodded that I understood. Just remembering the look on my dad's face when we got back on shore was the worst punishment that anybody could have given me.

STEP #8:
Beg Forgiveness

I couldn't go to sleep. Usually, I count fish. That's what Tina and I do instead of counting sheep. But fish were the last thing I wanted to think about tonight.

I lay in the dark, trying to forget about what had happened today.

I knew that Tina was thinking about it, too.

"I'm sorry about the fishing trip," I said.

"You ruined it for everybody," Tina said. "Why did you do such a dumb thing?" she asked.

"I told you. Because I wanted to catch a fish as big as Teddy's," I said.

Tina didn't say anything for a while. I thought for a moment that she was asleep.

"I guess I understand," Tina said with a yawn. Her yawn made me yawn. Then she yawned again and started to giggle. Sometimes Tina and I play the yawning game. One of us will yawn and the other one will do it, too. I knew that playing the yawning game was Tina's way of telling me that she accepted my apology.

"Good night, Willie." Tina yawned again. But this time her yawn was real.

Everything was quiet. The only sound in the house came from downstairs, where my parents were watching a TV movie. I thought about going down and telling them I was sorry. But then I knew that they'd probably be mad that I wasn't asleep yet.

I thought about Doofus Doolittle. I'd gone to bed without giving him a hug or even checking his food and water. I got up and slipped on my robe and house shoes. Very quietly, I walked down the hall.

I stopped for a moment outside of the study. If Teddy was awake, I could go in and tell him I was sorry for what had happened today.

"Teddy?" I said in a soft voice. I heard a noise, but when I knocked he didn't answer.

"Teddy?" I said again.

I opened the door slowly. Teddy was sitting on the edge of the bed. He was coughing softly, and he was wheezing. It sounded as if he couldn't catch his breath.

For a minute I didn't know what to do. Then I ran to the side of the bed and looked for Teddy's inhaler. But I couldn't find it. I could tell Teddy was really scared. He was as scared as I'd been in the lake today when I couldn't turn around. Teddy pointed to his suitcase. I went through the clothes in his suitcase, throwing everything on the floor until I found the inhaler. I rushed it to Teddy.

He put it into his mouth and began to breathe the medicine in.

I took his hand in mine and held it. "You're okay, Teddy. I'm going to get my parents," I said, and when he nodded, I ran downstairs to tell them what had happened. Both of my parents came running upstairs as fast as they could. Tina woke up and came into the room. My mother gave him some medicine, and soon he was breathing like he always does. I knew he was feeling much better.

"Sure you're okay, Teddy?" my dad asked.

"Yeah, I'm fine." Teddy looked a little embarrassed by all the attention.

My dad gave me a hug. "Good work, Willie. I'm proud of you," he said. "You knew what to do in an emergency."

My parents stayed around for a minute or two more to make sure that Teddy was okay. Finally, they went back downstairs and Tina went back to bed.

"Thank you, Willie," Teddy said after everybody had left. "I really get scared when I get my asthma."

"What does it feel like?" I asked.

"It feels like an elephant is sitting on

my chest and won't let me breathe," Teddy said. "It made me feel better to know that you were there."

"Even though I'm just a kid like you?" I asked him.

"You're my cousin, Willie, and that's more than being just a kid," he said.

"Sometimes I pretend that you and Tina are my sisters, and that you're my little sister."

"For real?" I asked.

"For real," he said. "You still want me to show you how to fly my kite?" Teddy said before I left the room.

"Yeah!" I said. So many things had happened this week, I'd forgotten all about Teddy and his kite.

I felt good when I went back to bed. I was glad that I'd been able to help Teddy

when he needed it, and I was glad my dad was proud of me. And I was glad that Teddy remembered that he had promised to show me how to fly his kite!

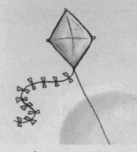

Step #9:
Go Fly a Kite

"This is a great place to fly a kite," Teddy said with a Teddy grin. We were standing in a field in the park near where I live. There were other kids with kites, too. My dad sat on a park bench reading the newspaper. Lydia's mom had taken Tina and Lydia to the mall. So it was just me and Teddy.

Teddy licked the tip of his finger and held it out. "The wind is really good. The most important thing about flying a kite is to have a good wind. The second-most important thing is to know what direction the wind is blowing," he said.

"Run with the kite until the wind catches it, and then let the string out until the kite sails," Teddy said.

"But you have to be careful you don't get it twisted up with anybody else's and you don't want to let it go. Here, you try it."

Teddy gave me his kite. I could tell how important the kite was to him. It made me feel good that he trusted me.

I did exactly what Teddy said to do, but his kite fell into the grass. I ran to pick it up, hoping it wasn't torn.

Teddy gasped. He picked the kite up and examined it. "Here. Try it again!" he said when he saw the kite was okay.

"No, Teddy. I'm scared it might fall again."

"Willie, it wasn't your fault. It was the wind's fault. Sometimes it comes, sometimes it doesn't. Go now! The wind is back!"

I took the kite, and I ran as fast as I could. I felt the wind pick it up and take it into the sky.

"Great!" I heard Teddy scream from behind me. Soon it was flying high in the sky.

"Great job, Willie! You really know how to fly that kite, don't you?" It was my dad's voice behind me.

"Thanks, Dad!" I said, but I was too busy making sure that Teddy's kite didn't get tangled with anybody else's to look at him. My dad gave me a pat on my shoulder.

The wind began to die down. Teddy's kite floated back to the ground.

"The wind is back; do you want to try it again?" Teddy asked.

"Sure," I said, and before I knew it, I was back in the clouds again, floating as high as Teddy's kite would take me.

Because it was Teddy's last night at our house, we had a special dinner, but this time there were enough fried chicken legs for everybody. My aunt was coming early the next morning to pick him up. We would be asleep when Teddy left, so my mom told Tina and me to say good-bye before we went to bed.

We knew we would be seeing Teddy again soon, so we weren't sad, but we gave him big hugs anyway.

Teddy was gone by the time Tina and I woke up the next morning. But we found two packages from Teddy wrapped in newspaper sitting on the end of our beds.

Tina's gift was the good-luck charm Teddy used to catch his fish, along with a note:

Dear Tina,
I've got three more, and I thought you might need it next time you go fishing.

As I started to unwrap my present, Doofus Doolittle surprised me and jumped up onto the bed. He snuggled into my lap and started purring.

My gift was Teddy's kite. Printed in huge letters across the top it said,

For Wonderful Willie when she wants to fly high, from Teddy.

It was one of the best gifts I'd ever gotten. Even better, Doofus Doolittle was back and licking my nose.

Okay, so I wrecked the kite. Teddy had it for three years. I have it for one day, and **SLAM–WHAM**! It gets reduced to a pile of orange paper, sticks, and string. One moment, I'm running and flying it higher, and higher, and higher, and the next thing I know, it's wrapped around a tree.

My dad and I spent the rest of the day taping, gluing, and tying it back together. But we lost most of the words in Teddy's message. So now it reads, "Wonderful Teddy."

The kite looks nothing like it did before. But I love to fly "Wonderful Teddy" every chance I get.

At dinner that day, my mom told me that I'm joining the Brownies. (She hopes I'll learn to be more responsible.) I just want to sell cookies! Who cares about cranky, old Mrs. Cotton when you've got a carton of cookies in the house?

Willie

Willimena, a Girl Scout?
Find out what happens in . . .
WILLIMENA RULES
How to Lose Your
Cookie Money
Rule Book #3